CASPER
A SPIRITED BEGINNING ™

Adapted by Amy Edgar
From the Screenplay
Written by Jymn Magon & Thomas Hart

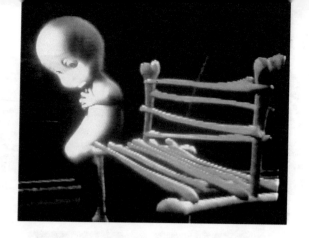

A ghost train sped through the dark night.

"This is not happening," said Casper, as a passenger flew by his seat. "I thought people only flew in dreams. Hey, that's it—I must be having a nightmare."

Casper asked another ghostly passenger where they were going. Annoyed, the ghost threw Casper right out the train window!

Casper landed with a thud, but quickly picked himself up. Scared and alone, he looked up and saw a sign that read: Welcome to Deedstown.

"Hope someone here can help me," said Casper.

"Pardon me, sir," he said to the grocer, "but I'm new here and . . ."

"A G-G-Ghost!" yelled the man and ran away.

Casper looked around but he didn't see a ghost. The next people he saw screamed and ran away, too. "Oh, no!" said Casper. "I'm a ghoooost!"

In a house nearby, Mike Carson and his son Chris were having breakfast.

"Hey, Dad," said Chris, "will you please come to the Open House at school tonight? I want you to meet my teacher, Miss Fistergraff, and to see my ghost poster."

"Sure, I'll come right after I tear down the old Applegate place," he answered. "It's the first phase of my plan to renovate this town."

"Don't forget about tonight, Dad!" shouted Chris as his dad ran out the door.

At the Applegate Mansion, a demolition crew was ready to tear down the building. But a group of rowdy protesters blocked the way of the bulldozers—they wanted to save the old building.

During the commotion, three ghosts appeared on the mansion's roof.

"Gang way, fleshies, we're comin' through!" the Ghostly Trio shouted.

People screamed as Stinkie breathed his stinky ghost breath on the crowd. Fatso wrapped up one protester like a mummy, and Stretch pulled another's underwear up over his head in a giant wedgie. The protesters and work crew took off running as fast as they could.

"Boys, the world is our oyster," said Stretch gleefully to the rest of the trio.

Not far away, a bully named Brock was picking on Chris. "Hey look, it's creepy Chris Carson," Brock said. "Off to another weirdo convention?" His friends laughed as he shoved Chris to the ground.

Just then, the scared protesters ran by yelling about ghosts. Brock and his friends took off running, too. But Chris recognized the work of the Ghostly Trio and headed right for the Applegate Mansion. Chris knew a lot about ghosts and even had a special book called The Ectoplasmic Britannica which explained all about ghosts and haunting.

Inside the mansion, Chris spotted the Ghostly Trio laughing about their latest scare. "Those people didn't stand a ghost of a chance," laughed Stinkie.

"Hey, guys, I know a lot about ghosts. Let me hang with you," said Chris.

"Us? Hang with a bag of bones? Don't make me laugh. Beat it!" yelled Stretch.

Feeling lonely, Chris left the mansion and headed for school.

Meanwhile the ghost train was pulling into Ghost Central Station. Snivel was the ghost in charge. "Welcome to our ghost train station. In other words, the place where you train to be ghosts—get it?" laughed Snivel. He counted the new ghosts as they stepped off the train. "Where's number 5?" he asked, checking his clipboard. "Where's Casper?"

Poor Snivel! He would have to tell the bad news to Kibosh, the fearsome green ghost in charge. "Excuse me for bothering you, Your Calmness, sir, but we're missing a ghost."

"We're what?" roared Kibosh. "I'm in charge here, and nobody skips training. Every ghost must go through the Ghost Processing Center to be trained properly. Now find him!"

At that moment the missing ghost was bumping into Chris Carson as he walked home from school. "Oops, sorry," said Casper. "Hey, wait a minute, you're not scared of me!"

"Of course not, I love ghosts," said Chris. "Bet it's fun—flying and vanishing."

"All I know is everyone just screams at me and runs away," said Casper, sadly.

"Let me guess," said Chris, "you feel like no one's on your side—like no one likes you?"

"Yeah," said Casper.

"I feel like that every day," said Chris. "We can be friends, and if you want to learn more about being a ghost, I know just who you need to see. Follow me!"

Casper and Chris entered the Applegate Mansion. "Who do we have here?" asked Stinkie.

"His name is Casper," said Chris. "He needs help learning how to be a ghost."

"Didn't they teach you anything at the ghost training center?" Fatso asked Casper. "Well, we'll teach you all our tricks and treats."

"Now the first thing you gotta learn is stealth mode. Just think clear thoughts—like wind," said Stretch. Casper concentrated very hard and disappeared for a few seconds.

"Not bad. See you later, fleshie," the ghost trio said to Chris. "We've got work to do."

Next the trio tried to teach Casper to fly by carrying him high in the air and letting him go. But instead of gliding, Casper fell like a stone. Then they tried to teach him to go through a wall, but he got stuck halfway and they had to pull him out by his tail.

Snivel spied on all that was going on at the mansion and called Kibosh. "Master, the Ghostly Trio is teaching Casper their unorthodox and, may I add, illegal ghostly techniques."

Kibosh flew into a rage and sent a bolt of electricity down the phone line that zapped Snivel to a frazzle. Ouch! "Those Halloweenies can't out-teach me!" yelled Kibosh.

"Good thing I'm already dead," groaned Snivel, "or that would have killed me."

The next morning, Chris was angry with his dad. "Dad, you totally missed my open house! I was the only kid without a parent!"

"I'll make it up to you," apologized Mike Carson. He promised Chris they would spend time together that night. Their "Wild and Crazy Guys" night would include a real sit-down dinner and a trip to the batting cage. Chris cheered up and raced to his room to grab his books for school.

Casper was waiting for him.

"I'm a lousy ghost," said Casper. "I'm just no good at being scary. The Ghostly Trio gave up on me."

"If those three losers won't help you, I will!" said Chris. "Come on Casper, we're going to school!"

Casper tried his best to learn from his new teacher.

"The first lesson is going through walls," said Chris. Casper tried so hard, he went through several walls at once. Oops! He went through the bathroom wall and scared the principal right off the toilet!

Next, Chris taught him how to change shape when he smuggled him into the library in his backpack. Casper was learning quickly.

Their haunting lessons were soon interrupted. "Who you talkin' to, space cadet?" asked Brock.

Suddenly, an invisible Casper grabbed the fire extinguisher off the wall and hooked it onto Brock's shirt. White foam went all over everything and everyone—including the principal. Brock was in big trouble now!

Casper finally felt good about himself. He flew off to try out his new powers and spotted a mean-looking man heading into the Shop and Save. The man was carrying a gun. In minutes, Casper scared him off and saved the store owner.

"From now on," said Casper happily, "I'll use my powers to help people. I want to be their friend."

Meanwhile, Mike Carson hired the only man in town who was not afraid of ghosts to demolish the mansion. Bill Case was an ex-military man who seemed a little crazy—it was his idea to blow-up the mansion with a bomb instead of knocking it down the usual way. In secret agent fashion, he crawled underneath the mansion and set the bomb to explode at 6:30 a.m.

Excited about spending a night with his dad, Chris decided to prepare a special dinner. Casper helped him iron some "grilled" cheese sandwiches and make some messy mashed potatoes.

   When his dad arrived home, Chris took him up to his room to meet Casper, but Casper wasn't there. Unknown to Chris, the Ghostly Trio had kidnapped him!

   Chris' father told him he had an overactive imagination and stormed out of the house. "Casper, how could you?" cried Chris.

   Upset, Chris decided to run away. He was walking along sadly when he bumped into Brock and the others. Still mad at Chris for getting him into trouble at school, Brock grabbed Chris and carried him to the Applegate Mansion. There, he and his friends locked Chris in a closet.

   "Sleep tight, don't let the dead bugs bite," called Brock as they left him alone in the scary mansion for the night.

Early the next morning, Mike Carson discovered his son had run away. As he frantically searched for Chris, he bumped right into Casper! After he got over the fright of meeting a real ghost, Casper told him that Chris was probably at the Applegate Mansion. Mike was horrified because he knew the mansion was scheduled to blow up in just a few minutes!

Outside the house, he ran into Miss Fistergraff who gave him a speedy ride to the mansion. Unable to convince Bill to stop the bomb, they raced inside the mansion, calling for Chris.

Casper quickly showed them the way, and they rescued Chris in the nick of time.

"I didn't mean to doubt you, son," said Mike. "I love you."

"I love you, Dad," Chris said, hugging him.

Inside the mansion, Casper noticed that the bomb was still ticking with only seconds to go before the mansion would be destroyed. Quickly, he started to eat the dynamite. As he finished, Kibosh and Snivel arrived. Kibosh grabbed Casper, and then:

KABOOM!

Casper expanded into a huge balloon that filled up the entire mansion.

"H-H-How did you do that?" gasped Kibosh.

"They taught me, sir," said Casper pointing at the Ghostly Trio. Impressed, Kibosh declared that the trio would be Casper's family for all time.

Mike, Chris, and Miss Fistergraff walked back into the mansion. Now they all wanted to save the old building. "If it were a haunted house, tourists would love it," suggested Miss Fistergraff.

The Ghostly Trio suddenly appeared. They were just the ghosts for the job. "A haunted house of our very own?" they asked. "You fleshies are the greatest."

"I think Casper will be a good influence on the Ghostly Trio," said Chris. "Because he's so friendly."

"Hey, I like the sound of that: Casper the Friendly Ghost!" Casper giggled. "Boo!"